FOUND SON

Thomas C.

SHAWN NICOLE PUBLISHING

Hartsdale, NY

Found Son; Any person whom has decided to walk in a positive manner.

Acknowledgments

My grandfather Thomas "Sonny" Blake, Yvonne Cox (Rip), Harlem 111th Street. So many people my family, friends just everyone who believed in me thanks.

Special Shout-Outs

Ms. Elizabeth Blake, MS. Wilimina Burks, Erika Denise Cors(Rip), Kellie Cors, All my children, My wife, nieces and nephews, Shaft Demby, Gene Rufus, Mutee, Donna DMC, S.L, Charles Mccants, Chip(Jahmil), Harbor fields(Big Lou)Brother B,(111th ST), everybody much love and respect, Kenny McKenzie, Drexel Ave, Michele/Charles Elliott, Joseph Cors.

Extra Thanks and Shout-Outs

Mikal Davis (Gabriel) Hold your head, thanks for the pointers on writing thanks.

PREFACE

B ig "L" has the coke game on lock in "A"-Town, but things are getting too hot for him in the streets. He has to devise a plan, to keep his deal with the Italian mafia, if not it could cost his family their lives.

Found Son is a fast-paced short story about the lies, betrayal, sex, mayhem. That corrupts so many young minds into believing the streets are their reality. Nevertheless, most of all it is about redemption.

THE BEGINNING

I t all started about 1985. We were all young kids, with a whole lot of time on our hands. I can remember he use to come jogging through the block, always joking saying some funny shit to make you laugh. His name was Big "L" and man was he quick! He would be running backwards and frontward throwing jabs we would say look at this dude go!

CHAPTER 1

Before we jump too far ahead, let us start from the very beginning. It was around February 1971, a little boy was born in the Bronx, New York. From a young child, I guess you could say he was always observing everything, and everyone around him. This little boy had an imaginary friend, he would tell him "One day, I will have everything this world has to offer."

The young boy's name was Tarsi and his mother's name was Tichele, in grade school Tarsi was very good with numbers, math was his favorite subject. Tichele had Tarsi young and even though Tarsi never knew his biological father. The dad he had known raised him, and gave Tarsi his last name. Tichele married this cat; named Cuba he was a very intelligent dude, he just applied his skills to all the wrong shit.

One of the things Cuba taught Tarsi, was how to take care of himself. "Cuba would say you need a book education, a street education." In addition, Cuba told Tarsi treat everyone including your enemy, the way you want to be treated.

Cuba owned a couple of corner stores, Tarsi worked in both stores as a child. This alone was getting him very popular in the neighborhood. Nevertheless, something else was happening hustlers, pimps, were grooming him and last but not least a very dangerous hit man from D.C named Big Mu. However, like I said this was everyday life for Tarsi.

CHAPTER 2

B ig "L" comes jogging threw the block one afternoon, sees Tarsi, and his friend's break dancing.
Big "L" screams out "Hey Yo! Tarsi I want you to
meet my little sister." Tarsi was excited that "L" had even
noticed him. Also Tarsi thought nothing else of L's offer
to meet his little sister, he wasn't even into girls yet. Tarsi
had a hard but cool life, his mom worked very hard.
Cuba his step-pops did whatever he did to put food on
the table.

So finally, the day has come for Tarsi to meet Big L's
little sister, her name was Crystal. In addition, let me tell
you when Tarsi first seen her; it was love at first sight.
Every night they sat on the phone for hours, falling
asleep on the phone. Crystal's mom was always yelling,

saying "That fast ass little boy is going to get your little ass in trouble one day."

Laughing Crystal would whisper, "My mom is just jealous because you love me so much". So Big "L" sees Tarsi one day and says, "Listen little man I want you to take Crystal to the movies for her birthday. " Tarsi cracks up and say, "I would love to "L" but my allowance is not enough for us to ride the bus to the movies."

Big "L" says "don't worry little homie I got you, I will give you some paper" I just want Crystal to enjoy her birthday.

Now when I tell you this shit was too much for little Tarsi to handle. Tarsi started thinking to himself; "shit I would carry L's boxing shoes to the gym in the pouring rain."

Furthermore, Tarsi could not believe he was even going to the movies with a girl, and it was Big L's little sister! Now see this shit was better than hitting the lottery. So now, it was the day of the movies date, a horn is blowing. Ms. Tichele looks outside her window asking? "Who is this making all this damn noise in front of my house?" Being as nosey as she naturally was. She looks outside; there is this brand new blue BMW 750i sitting front of her door.

Tichele yells upstairs, to Cuba thinking this is one of his friends. "Cuba who the hell is that?" Cuba answers "I don't know that young kid, why are you asking me."

The young boy in the car "yells out excuse me is Tarsi home?" Can you please tell him it's "L." Ms. Tichele goes in Tarsi's room fuming asking? Why is this grown man in a BMW asking for you?"

Tarsi run to the door and starts laughing, he explains moms relax; "that's Crystal and her big brother "L," we're going to the movies." Mom remember I told you that a couple of days ago. Ms. Tichele is looking with suspension saying to herself "how can this young boy afford such an expensive car?"

Nevertheless, she did not want to jump to any conclusions maybe she should have if she knew the road her baby boy was about to travel.

Now back to the movie date everything had went perfect; Crystal loved her new "boo" Tarsi. On top of that, the whole school knew, Tarsi had taken Crystal out so his popularity had grown tremendously.

Not only was Tarsi getting popular in school, he was also getting cool with older dudes in the neighborhood. Because unbeknown to him Big "L" was a real boss, I mean Cuba did not have shit on "L"! Yeah Cuba was moving crazy pounds of weed no doubt! However, this nigga "L" was moving crazy weight meaning keys, bricks of coke seriously this dude was a giant in the coke game.

CHAPTER 3

Cuba's weed business is booming right now and he has big plans. Cuba was working on one of the largest marijuana shipments to come through "A" town. It is rumored that Satan himself owns "A" town, rents it for a small price the souls of "A" towns children."

Yeah so, things are looking very good for Cuba I mean the weed is flying off the shelves. There used to be trash bags full of money pounds, and pounds of weed in the closets. It used to take Ms. Tichele 2 to 3 days, to count all the cash in the crib. Shit was crazy for real, the neighborhood where they sold the weed was quiet, and had hard working families.

Most of them use to buy their weed or sold weed for Cuba. One thing everybody knew each other, it was real love. Cuba's two stores were more than what they appeared to be they were a front. Cuba was the weed man in the hood, being a naive little boy Tarsi never paid any attention to how his parents made their living. Even though, now that you look back "Tarsi had shit other kids in the neighborhood couldn't afford."

CHAPTER 4

Okay, so Tarsi is starting to hear his name in the streets, people are whispering. Older people are starting to give Tarsi his props; Tarsi did not yet understand, he is being sized up. One day Crystal comes over Tarsi house, asks him do you need some new sneakers?

Tarsi hesitate for a minute; then asked? "Where are you getting the money from, for new sneakers?" Crystal laughs and answers, "Boy my brother always gives me money." Crystal was not Big L's real sister her oldest sister Tasha was his girlfriend and Tasha, (L) gave Crystal anything she wanted.

High school was the spot if you were book smart, had nice things you're accepted. Therefore, after school one day, Crystal and Tarsi were walking to the bus stop, Crystal's older sister Tasha pulls up.

She tells both kids, "Look what "L" bought me," Now when I tell you this car she was pushing was crazy, it was a smoked grey Maserati, with grey Gucci interior. But only if Tarsi would have only seen these hating ass "old heads" sitting at the traffic light, seeing all this big boy shit going down.

He would have understood, why the events that took place in his life went the way they did.

One late night Big Mu the hit man from Northeast D.C; comes in the store and tells Tarsi "listen little man real bad boys move in silence." Mu also goes onto to say, "A real nigga never tells" If you in this life, do some shit, should catch a case; own up to your shit. With all of this, Tarsi had a lot racing through his head. Overnight, it seems Tarsi have a new girlfriend, making things more complicated, Mu schooling him how to make moves.

CHAPTER 5

Ms. Tichele came from a very hard working family; her mom worked for the Government (Feds), her dad was a big hat for a major beer distributor. The story is supposed to have gone like this. When Tichele got pregnant with Tarsi she got her heart broke, so this made her leave New York. In addition, being her father's child he gave her a choice; get married or sign the child over to him. Her dad felt with option #2 she could live her life, live her dreams. However, of course she took the hard route, which led to some bumpy ass situations.

Ms. Tichele had two more children two daughters. The oldest daughter her name is Denise, the baby of the family her name was Krae. When they came into the world they were Tichele, Cuba; everything, and life was still stable. Cuba was still getting that paper he was neck deep in the weed game.

Nevertheless, shit was not quite the same anymore. Because somebody introduced that crack "rock" to "A" town.

Cuba started complaining about how the money was not right, him and Ms. Tichele were arguing over everything. In addition, things were changing in Cuba's crew also; I think the crew was starting to sense a sign of weakness about Cuba.

One night Cuba "told Mu if shit gets any worst we might have to start robbing other hustlers." Mu just smiled and said "you know that's my shit anyway," murder and torture was some kind of sickness this dude loved. However, one thing about Mu; even though was a straight killer. He loved Cuba and his family; he would have massacred anyone trying to bring harm to them.

Cuba was bugging out; acting fucking crazy and the stores were starting to look empty nothing like in the beginning. The selves use to be stocked with all the good snacks like sour pickles in the bag, Lemon Heads, Boston baked beans, pop rocks, sodas, chips all that good shit just thinking about it makes you get the munchies.

What was crazy Cuba was cool with everybody in the block. I mean all of Tarsi's friends their moms and pops were starting to hang at the crib even the fucking mail carrier. Tarsi and his little sisters would wake up "one" two" o'clock in the morning and find somebody from the neighborhood in the kitchen beaming up. Then you had that horrible ass smell I mean this shit would make u sick it stunk so badly.

However, being little kids Tarsi and his sisters did not know; that smell was crack "rock" being smoked.

Cuba and Big Mu one day were disgusting there weed business when unexpected Cuba tells Big Mu look "I am finished I am out the game."

Big Mu is furious; he says, "What the fuck do you mean? You're finished what? Cuba "went on to say he could not do it anymore"; he was giving up the hustling life. This made Big Mu very upset he starts to yell, "motherfuckers are you fucking crazy we have a good thing going here".

Cuba just stares as if in some kind of trance and Big Mu goes on to ask? "Why are your eyes so glassy Cuba talk to me man" I know you not doing what the fuck I think you are doing and there was silence.

Then out of nowhere Big Mu, this deranged killer breaks down and starts crying and sobbing like a little child. What no one knew Cuba had saved Mu from the streets when he was a young boy? Yeah Big Mu was a homeless heroin addicted kid lost wondering the streets of D.C., when he first met Cuba; Cuba was the only person to show him any love.

In fact, Cuba got Mu off the heroin; told him to take up a hobby and master it. Then will you find your calling in life.

Big Mu took his advice, after doing a bid in juvenile detention joint in Prince George County Maryland. Mu was ready to take on his new lifestyle.

CHAPTER 6

B ig "L" is training hard; he has a big fight coming up, he has to be in top shape to defeat Breon "Leroy" Jackson. Breon was the number one contender in the country. One afternoon Tarsi and Crystal are sitting on her sister's front porch, when two Italian dudes pull up in this "Black Phantom."

One of them approaches the kids and asks? "Is there were Big L lives?" Tarsi looks at Crystal and "she kindly asks sir" If you do not mind may I ask who wants to know? The bigger of the two said yes, "could you please let "L" know Mr. Bruno from New York is here about his boxing career." Not thinking anything of it Tarsi gets up, runs inside, and tells "L" he has company.

Mr. Bruno you remember the boxing promoter, well he did more than just promote fights. He represented some major players in the cocaine distribution circle of friends. See A-town had a reputation for having hustlers and plenty of junkies; the Italians just needed someone who they felt had the brains and heart to pull off the job, after a couple of business meetings between Mr. Bruno, Big "L" it was on.

By this time Big "L" had the whole "A" town on lock, if you were moving coke most likely you were selling (L's) coke, even if you didn't know you were. Shit was crazy there used to be so much money "L" had two safes the size of a refrigerators stuffed packed with paper.

CHAPTER 7

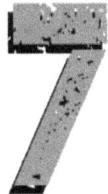

One night Crystal comes over Tarsi's crib, nothing new same as usual. However, something different was about to happen they start to kiss and grinding Tarsi is sucking on her nipples, Crystal is sucking on Tarsi's neck.

Then Tarsi un-zippers Crystal jeans and puts his fingers in her pants and starts playing with her pussy. "They are acting like two dogs in heat." Tarsi sticks, his finger in that tight "wet pussy" she is moaning going crazy.

Then Tarsi slide his pants off, and then take Crystal's pants off, puts her legs back into a pretzel position, and slides that "hammer" inside of her. "Oh my God" she is screaming, telling him not to stop, I mean for it to be both of their first times they were getting it the fuck in.

Young Tarsi is killing the pussy straight murdering it, and then he feels something he never felt before. He is thinking damn this shit is intense but feels good as fuck! Crystal asks baby what is wrong. Tarsi can barely speak; he just rolls his eyes up in his head, lets the hot thick lava flow. Crystal and Tarsi had done the mother fucking thing, yep she gave him some sex; thinking to himself that shit was good.

Only if someone would have told them to take their time, do not rush their lives. As time went on, Crystal starts to notice some shit changing about her. She was sleeping more, eating more. Until one day Tasha went, to pick up Tarsi she says; "I think my sister is pregnant" if you could have seen the look on Tarsi face. You would have thought he saw a ghost, now things are starting to get real!

Tarsi went to one of his older cousins that lived in the neighborhood, to ask what he should do. His cousin's name was Big "O" "his cousin starts laughing, after hearing the story. He tells "get a fucking abortion, Big "O" goes on to say "little cousin you are too young for that shit right now".

Not knowing which way to turn, Tarsi tells Ms. Tichele, she goes crazy. I mean she is flipping the fuck out, she must have called, Tarsi every "stupid mother-fucker in the book."

She was throwing shit at him, now thinking back Tarsi "still cracks up laughing" when he thinks about his past. She went ballistic. After Ms. Tichele calms down, she hugs her son; "says baby the best thing for both of you is an abortion."

Ms. Tichele goes on to explain, "How she had a child young," how hard everything was for her. However, Crystal being the chicken head she was, she is stuck on keeping her baby. As time went on Crystal's stomach grew larger and larger, so did her appetite she was greedy as hell.

In addition, her attitude was to the point her own mother could no longer stand the sight of her, one day Crystal's mom said "Crystal I love you, but you have to go" it is time you lived on your own. "I can't take your bullshit any more just get the fuck out!

"Crystal cried, said "mommy I promise I will change." Nevertheless, her cries went on deaf ears, the truth Crystal's mother had her first baby when she was 12, her conscious was eating at her for her own bullshit. One Saturday night Tarsi went to visit Crystal; she breaks down and broke the news. "Tarsi my mom said I have to leave, "she starts to cry," Where I'm suppose to go?"

Crystal continues to say, "I don't have any money and I am too young to get a place. " Crystal begs, "Tarsi please baby help me, I am scared what have we done", they both just hugged each other and cried; Tarsi tells himself "I have to ask my mom if Crystal can stay with us."

CHAPTER 8

One late night, at Cuba's house there was this loud ass knock on the door, whomever it was banging frantically. "Let me the fuck in," I am bleeding badly, "Mu was yelling. " I have been shot," the crazy thing this happened after doing a hit for Cuba. Come to find out that night, Big Mu had just finished hitting someone up, just so happens one of his crews rival was lying in the cut, ready to return the favor. Karma is a bitch.

Nevertheless, the Devil was not finished with Big Mu yet, he survived his injuries. Now, that Cuba has said what is on his mind, this sends Mu into a rage. All Mu is thinking "if Cuba gives everything up", how he might return to using heroin or worst end up homeless, with his past lingering.

Mu does the unthinkable, he sees a dude who owed an old drug debt; Mu had seen this dude a 100 times since this debt occurred, never said anything more than "what's good my dude". However, today this dude would never see his family again, acting off his emotions. Big Mu waited, for the person to be out of sight of everyone, shoots him once in the temple, Big Mu continued on his way thinking; just another fool in the dirt. Not knowing a woman witnessed the whole murder from her bedroom window. Nevertheless, being scared the woman never came forward fearing the killer would retaliate. Until one day, the woman who witnessed the murder, was riding the bus, out of nowhere a woman sits beside her. This woman begins to say, how today was very sad for her.

Therefore, this stranger on the bus just continues, says today marked her son's fifth death anniversary. The witness could not believe what she was hearing and being nosey, she continued to lend a listening ear. Therefore, the woman goes on to say, "someone murdered her baby in broad daylight" and no one seemed to see anything, hearing this was really starting to bother the woman; who witnessed the murder 5 years ago.

Because she knew herself, she had not done the right thing by reporting what she had witnessed. The witness asked out of curiosity. "Where did your son get murdered Ms." The mother answers on the corner of Hill Ave. "Oh? My God" the witness is thinking, she started doing the math in her head. Five years ago, Hill Ave. "Please Lord forgive me," "I witnessed this woman's child get murdered" and did not do anything please forgive me father!

Back to the woman on the bus, so she continues to talk about "her son's death."

Moreover, the woman who witnessed the crime is saying in her mind "what should I do?" I witnessed who killed this woman's son; after five years, she decides to call the Detective's office, the phone rings ring ring! The voice on the other end answers, says, "Hello Detective Corbin speaking", "in a calm detective voice how may I help you?"

There is silence between them for a minute, "Hello Detective Corbin repeats." The witness answers; "hello detective my name is there is silence, "I would rather not answer that right now sir I am really scared." Detective Corbin replies no problem "how can we help what seems to be the problem?" The witness mumbles something "there was a murder about 5 years ago on Hill Ave.," then she begins to panic" sorry sir I have to go.

Wait, Detective Corbin yells; "stay on the phone with me" and relax what did you see? The witness answers, "I know who killed that man on Hill Ave." Detective

Corbin says, "Stay still, I am sending a car to pick you up right away!"

Once the witness arrives at the station house, the Detective greets her. "Hello Miss can I get you anything?"

"Just promise me I won't be killed; the woman answers" "And you catch the bastard that committed this horrible crime."

After the witness came forward, the cops now had everything they needed to put Big Mu away for life. The cops have suspected Mu in a couple dozen murders. However, never were able to produce any witness. Now with Big Mu behind bars for the rest of his natural life, things really start to spiral downhill for Cuba.

CHAPTER 9

L ate one night, while taking a walk with his mother, Tarsi decided it is time to tell Ms. Tichele the news. He asked. "Mom, how would you feel if I had a baby coming?" Moreover, before he could finish his question "She said I would kill your little ass. " Tarsi starts to think; "This shit is going to be harder than I thought." Furthermore, she went on to say "I know it better not be by Crystal". That night it was complete silence between them and the next day. Tarsi were scared to death; he did not know what to do.

Another night, Tarsi says, "Mom I have something else serious to talk to you about" "Ms. Tichele asks what now?" What could be more serious than what you have already said to me? "Well Crystal's mom said she has to move out." "Ms. Tichele cuts him before he could finish oh hell"! "You must have really lost your mind," Ms. Tichele continues to say"; Tarsi I know you not asking me, if this little bitch can stay in my house." "Please mom Tarsi begged," I will help out with the bills, we will stay in school." Please mom she is having my baby your grandchild.

"Ms. Tichele said you must really be fucking retarded and furthermore how do you even know that's your baby?"

"Did you even think about that with your little dumb ass?" Tarsi did not pay his moms ranting any attention, about the baby not being his. Tarsi knew his mother "was just upset and disappointed with Crystal," because she this had messed her son's life up. Tarsi pressed his luck, begs one last time "please mom just think about it." After making these promises, Tarsi really had to put on his thinking cap. Therefore, in the beginning Tarsi kept his promise, he stayed in school, got a job roasting peanuts, do not laugh at least he had a job.

One day Tarsi had seen Big 'L', he "said sorry little man," "I heard Crystal's mom flipped out on her," "how are things holding up"? Tarsi said it is hard; we will be all right though, "L" admired Tarsi's attitude. In addition, "L" could see Tarsi was growing up, maybe ready to join the business. So Big "L" did not want to apply too much pressure he told Tarsi "here is a couple of dollars, if you need anything else call me."

Tarsi went home, told Crystal I just saw L, "he asked how you were?" In addition, he gave us a couple of dollars, when Tarsi opened the bag him, Crystal just looked at each other. Like are you fucking serious, it was 5000.00 (Five thousand dollars).

They both yelled, Tarsi said this is more money he had ever seen; Crystal was used to seeing paper like that. Now, it is on, Tarsi went to school; all the other little dudes were pulling out there little knots of money, Tarsi pull out a stack of hundreds just to buy a slice of pizza. "He was on his big boy shit real heavy."

Things are looking beautiful and Ms. Tichele finally lets Crystal move in, after a while Ms. Tichele is starting to come around; both kids are going to school. In addition, Tarsi is working, Ms. Tichele figures she rather have them home. Then off in the streets somewhere, only if she had a crystal ball shit was about to go down in big kind of way.

CHAPTER 10

Crack has destroyed Cuba, he and Tichele have lost everything. Both stores are empty, he traded most of the weed he was selling for crack; I mean shit was really bananas right now for them. Ms. Tichele was working her ass off, to support the family and pay for Cuba's crack habit. Tichele is starting to think, enough is enough, and Cuba infested an entire neighborhood with crack, because he introduced this shit to the block where everything and everyone seemed normal.

People's lives were destroyed you had doctors, homemakers even the telephone man selling their souls for a hit off that 'glass dick'.

One night Tarsi hear his mother crying, he asks his mom what is wrong. "She answers baby nothing," Tarsi says mom talk to me what is wrong? She answers "baby we don't have any money and we might get evicted." Tarsi ask his mother "where are your paychecks." She just cried harder, she says son its time; "I tell you the truth"

"Tarsi is boiling mad; as he just listens, as Ms. Tichele goes on to say "all my money either Cuba is smoking it up and the rest I am paying the Jamaicans back." Tarsi is confused, very angry he ask "what Jamaicans, mom what are you talking about?"

Tichele goes to explain, "When Cuba was on top, in the weed game." Some Jamaicans had given him a shipment of 20000 lbs. of weed on consignment, Tarsi "I should not be talking to you about this shit." "No mom please, I want to know everything continues." Ok baby "Ms. Tichele replied when Cuba got addicted to crack he owed the Jamaicans $50,000 dollars and now they want to collect."

Tichele goes on saying, "to make things worst they know how much money I make. " Because they have inside contacts at my job, they are demanding $3,000.00 a month, until all their money paid in full. Again, Ms. Tichele starts sobbing even harder, Tarsi; "Screams what mom what the fuck those curry goat eating mother fucker said to you?" Sobbing out of control, "she whispered they said they are going to kill the whole house if I miss one payment.

CHAPTER 11

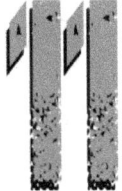

Saturday comes around, Tarsi go to work to pick-up his first paycheck, he looks inside the envelope and is saying to himself; "What is this bullshit." He is thinking Big "L" had just given him 5000.00 dollars for nothing; here he is busting his ass. "Roasting peanuts for peanuts," sweating like a runaway slave. He takes his apron off and says, "Hey boss man I quit"; "I am out of here time to get some real paper.

Tarsi is thinking; "I have this baby coming, I need some real money. Therefore, he makes that call, Big "L" answers, "hey what's good, Tarsi is everything cool?" Tarsi answer "yeah "L", "listen man I wanted to thank you", for always looking out for me and Crystal. Big "L" responds no problem we family little brother, Tarsi goes on to say, "Well "L" I do need to ask you something.

Big 'L' "says talk to me what's good little brother, what's on your mind?" Tarsi hesitates for a minute, then tells "L" I am ready to make some real paper" "L" just listens to Tarsi talk; L always dug Tarsi's style to be such a young boy. Big "L" says, "I will pick you up later I'm picking up my new car."

Tarsi is very nervous, he does not know what to say to Big L, Tarsi knows nothing about the streets. However, you see Big "L" was a real smart, he already knew, once he gave Tarsi that money it would not be long before he was calling him. In addition, "L" knew Tarsi did not know shit about the cocaine game, "L" already had a special job lined up for his little man.

That evening Crystal and Tarsi are chilling on the front porch, when this white Mercedes Benz S550 pulls up, Crystal whispers; "Tarsi that car, is fucking nice as hell damn." Tarsi just look in aw, as if damn that has to be some rich persons' shit. The tinted windows roll down, it Big "L" grinning, looking like the rich young nigga he was. Tarsi damn near died I mean this shit was unreal Big "L" said "hey! Crystal when is that baby dropping so I can spoil my little solider".

Then "L" asks Crystal, let me borrow Tarsi for a minute? Showing off, Big "L" asked Tarsi so what you think about the Benz? Tarsi says; Big "L" "you are the truth." Then Big "L" goes on to say, "I am glad you chose that word truth."

"Because little brother we have to always be truthful," I mean you can talk to me about anything. Even if you think, I might get angry.

Tarsi "says, "Big "L" I would never do anything to lose your trust, I love you man." "All right then" "L" says. "That's good because this is what I have in store for you." I want you to be around me, so you can see how I do things.

Before I expose you to the vicious ass world, we live in, Tarsi is being real patient keeping his composure. Tarsi just listen, agrees with Big L.

"Okay little brother this is the plan; at first you will come when I call you, sometimes I will give you a bag it's no need for you to know its contents. Just know you well get them 3-4 times a week, all you have to do is keep them in your house somewhere safe.

Either Tasha or I will come through and get them "that's it nothing more nothing less." Tarsi "says that is it," I want to do more, I want a nice car too. Big "L" laughs and says, "be easy your time well come just follow what I am telling you to do."

Big "L" "says "oh yeah, before I forget you well get $2,500.00 dollars for every bag you hold. So do the right thing with your paper, you will have that car in no time. Tarsi is dumfounded, he cannot believe what he just heard, came from nobody to a superstar. Come to think most dudes his age were hustling, getting sneaker money, maybe buying there girlfriend some earrings, Tarsi was making at least $20,000 a month, just stacking you do the math and he was only 15. As time passes, Seems Tarsi is better at hustling than originally anticipated.

Big "L" approaches Tarsi one late night and says, "Listen Tarsi things are getting a little hot for me," "I have to lay low for a little while." Tarsi is wondering, what could be possibly wrong. Big "L" tells Tarsi, "go see Tasha; she has some instructions for you."

Tarsi continue to say; "L" you are talking, as if. "I will not ever see you again." Big L just smiles, "says even when you do not see me," "I will see you and drives off." Okay, so a few days passed by, finally Tasha calls Crystal. "Hey little sister where is your baby daddy?" Tell him to meet me at Dino's house. Dino was one of "L" Lieutenants, another heavy weight in the streets. He used to move those bricks like a "construction company."

Hey, "Tarsi what is up with you," as she walked in Dino crib? Tarsi responds "nothing just trying to be safe out here," "you know it is either the cops or the stick up kids," then Tarsi says Tasha! "Fuck the small talk. What is Big "L" talking about; not seeing him for a while? Tasha answers "listen Tarsi "L" needs you, we all need you right now!"

Shit is crazy, Tasha goes on saying, Feds are on "L" someone has been snitching. Tarsi tells Tasha you know I am too ready to ride for my family. What is going on talk to me, Tasha says remember Mr. Bruno "L" boxing promoter from NY. Tarsi answers, "yeah why what's up did they do "L" dirty?" Tasha laughs, no boy they are the fucking mafia, she goes on saying they are the ones that have been giving "L" all that coke he has been selling.

Tarsi is just listening "thinking; what does this shit have to do with me?" Tasha goes on to say; "ok fuck it "L" had to cosign for you, he needed someone he could trust to keep his deal with the Italians." She tells Tarsi "see no matter what "L" has to move 100 kilos a month for them," In addition; being as though "L" has to disappear for a while, he needs someone to fill his spot with our friend Mr. Bruno.

Tarsi is just dumbfounded, 100 keys a month he is thinking; should I be happy or scared to death. Now Tarsi have to put together his own team, he is only 16 years old. Tarsi now think he owes what he thinks is the mafia's money a whopping 1.5 million dollars a month. How deceit can be so misleading.

The streets are crazy right now, I mean Tarsi, and his crews are supplying most of "A" town, the surrounding areas. In addition, Crystal has her second baby a little boy, so Tarsi takes Crystal, the kids. Buys them a nice little townhouse with a beach view everything is moving as planned.

CHAPTER 12

T arsi's face fills with anger; the more his mother tells him about her owing someone 50,000 dollars, even though he is young, his hand is strong in the streets. He contacts one of his cousin Tajuan, who calmed him down, said "little cousin" how do you want to handle this situation? Tarsi is thinking; he is so fucking angry, he almost killed Cuba with two shots to the head.

However, he knew his mom loved this nigga, no matter his shortcomings; he was Tarsi' dad after all. Tarsi tells his mother, "call them dudes and tell them, Friday come get there paper." Tarsi then tell his mother, do not give them cowards another nickel, also mom they not killing shit around here. Believe that. I have the money mom I got you.

Tichele, "looks up in tears," says "Tarsi what do you mean?" Tarsi "says mom I got the money don't worry about anything" Ms. Tichele is bugging out, "she asks you have what Tarsi?" Ms. Tichele did not know if she wanted to laugh or cry, she is thinking to herself; "the boy done want stalk raving mad." Moreover, Mr. Man "were the hell would you get $50,000 (fifty thousand dollars) from" his mom asked?

Tarsi says mom, I have to be honest and I have been doing my thing in these streets. We are straight with money right now; believe your son make the call. In addition, tell them I will deliver the money just name the time and the place.

Okay, so now Ms. Tichele knows her baby boy is making power moves, she starts to worry about him. Nevertheless, one thing does not change about her; she is spending that money with no problems. One night Tarsi call his mom, "I have a surprise for you mom." Ms. Tichele is looking at the phone blushing, thinking, "Like what has this boy did now." Tarsi press his mom's doorbell; Come outside mom, close your eyes and do not peek. "Ok moms open up." "Oh! My God" Tarsi, his mom screams tears streaming down her face. "Whose car is this baby"?

Tarsi just smiles, says "it's yours mommy", a special car for a special lady" happy birthday, Cuba fake ass smile on his face, you could see the jealousy. He was always jealous of Tarsi his own son, Cuba, use to spoil Ms. Tichele with lavish gifts, but nothing like a candy apple red Mercedes CL 550 coupe, with snow white interior and that big red bow on the hood! The only thing Ms. Tichele could say is my baby did it again, she starts crying and saying, "Tarsi, how did you know your mom's dream car?" Once again, Tarsi always laughing said," Mommy I know all your dreams."

However, the haters were plotting on her; what did you expect she is driving around, in the nicest Benz coupe in the city.

CHAPTER 13

One night Tasha asks Tarsi, "How is everything in the streets?" Tarsi reply shit is better than expected; the coke is flying off the shelves. Things are going good right now. Tarsi, asked, "Tasha what is up," "why did you ask me that"? Tasha looks at him and says, "I am just checking," I really appreciate the way you have looked after everything and me. Tarsi answer, "That is what family does, and we stick together."

Tasha gets word to Tarsi to meet her; she had some urgent information for him. Tarsi got the message, say no problem," tell Tasha I will meet her later tonight." So Tarsi is sitting by the playground, in his new Porsche Cayenne he just bought himself for his 18th birthday; it was nice, it was smoke grey, with light grey interior. Tasha pulls up and gets in.

"Hey Tarsi I see you making power moves, I like you in this Cayenne. " Then Tasha continues to say, what Tarsi never expected to hear. Tasha says listen" Tarsi ever since "L" left town I get fucking lonely," Tarsi laughed and ask you want me to hook you up with Shad?

They both bust out laughing, she says hell no nigga I don't fuck with the help," Tasha says seriously Tarsi I get lonely and horny.

By now Tarsi started to trip, not only is this "L" girl, this is Crystal's sister. Tarsi say, "Tasha I feel you," but before he could finish Tasha had her tongue down his throat. Tasha says "Tarsi I am so fucking sorry" then she goes on, "I am starting to look at you in a different way," and I want to be with you.

Tarsi is thinking to himself; "this is not happening", Tasha goes on saying; I never meant to hurt my sister. However, why the fuck should she have everything the houses, the kids, nice fucking cars and most of all you baby I love you Tarsi.

CHAPTER 14

Therefore, word gets back to this hustler named Black, Tarsi is the man, there is no one else, and with the quantity or quality of the product, he is moving.

In addition, Tarsi's prices were so good there is no need to see out of town connects anymore, to be a kid Tarsi was doing major things, back to Black word is, he supposed to be some kind of boss running a couple of projects in "A" Town.

Tarsi is not impressed, because Tarsi never dealt with anyone he did not know. Black sends word he wants a sit down with Tarsi. One night, while at the opera Tarsi asked his right hand man Shad; "who is this nigga Black" and how does he know who the fuck I am, Shad answers "some cat moving a couple of keys," nothing serious".

Yeah, Shad is Tarsi's right hand man and he was always talking slick out his mouth. Later that night, while driving home Tarsi tells Shad; "oh yeah fuck that nigga what's his name Black" Who the fuck is he, to want a sit down with me? Shad just laughs and "says fuck that nigga then.

The next day, Shad runs across the chick who gave the message. He gives her a stack of hundred dollar bills and tells her "check it shorty, no disrespect to you what's you name anyway?" She answers Mona, Shad replies "Ok cool, I well remember that but tell your man Black my man Tarsi don't do the sit down shit". Mona pops her gum and says "all right Shad" but Black does not like answers like that. She walked away, that entire ass was bouncing all over the place.

Damn Shad is thinking; damn Mona's ass is crazy, I would fuck the shit out of her. However, being Shad he snapped back to reality mind right back on business. Mona delivers the message; Black does not take the news to well, "he is thinking to himself." Oh word, this bitch ass nigga don't do meetings huh?"

Shad was flamboyant, he bought dumb shit, and it brought unnecessary attention. Shad was Tarsi's right hand man, but they were opposite attracted. For example, he brought a Rolls Royce Bentley. It is the summer, it is a Friday night, and Shad is on the other side of town.

He was going to check this little slim fine ass, young girl, he met at a basketball game, he pulls up in the projects in a brand mother fucking Bentley coupe. By now, the whole project is standing around, like whom the fuck is this person, in this nice ass Bentley. Nevertheless, see Tarsi did not like show boating and Shad was always slipping, doing some stupid shit. Now who in the fuck goes in the hood; even worst the fucking projects in a brand new Bentley coupe. Yep, you got it mother fucking Shad always thinking with his dick.

In addition, unbeknown to Tarsi this nigga Black had already had the wolves following Ms. Tichele around, now he got the drop on Shad driving around in this fucking two-hundred thousand dollar car.

So Shad calls Tarsi one night and says, "I had a run in with that nigga Black" when I was visiting this little bitch downtown. Tarsi says "yeah okay and what!" Shad goes on telling Tarsi," This nigga said "either you get down with him or Ms. Tichele won't make it home."

Now, why the fuck would Black say some dumb shit like that, the news sent Tarsi into a rage. I mean Tarsi is going crazy, literally "turning red." Tarsi say "enough with this silly rabbit," "He said what." Immediately Tarsi calls up his special bitch he keeps on speed dial just for special shit just like this.

CHAPTER 15

M s. Tichele calls, says "hey sugar come have dinner with your mommy" we have not sat down like a family in a long time. Tarsi says sure mom dukes, I need to talk to you anyway.

Tarsi arrives at his moms house, she cooked his favorite meal turkey, stuffing and mashed potatoes. Tarsi walks in, Cuba was on the sofa drunk and high from smoking crack all night.

Tarsi whispers to Cuba. "Cuba wake up man" Cuba jumps up startled, says, "Oh shit what brings your highness to visit us peasants." Tarsi just laughed that bullshit off; as if I told you, earlier Cuba was always jealous of Tarsi.

In addition, the messed up thing about it Cuba was the one who groomed Tarsi for this street shit. That is a hell of father for you anyway. Tarsi respond to Cuba's bullshit, "Dad you know I am busy but I love you." "Truthfully" Tarsi wished his pops would clean up his act, so he could put him down. Cuba was one hell of a hustler back in his day. After dinner, Tarsi tell his mom "something serious has come up," Ms. Tichele starts to look worried she says, "What is wrong baby"? , Tarsi go on to say mom "shit is very hectic for me out in these streets and things might get a little bit crazy."

Tarsi says "mom I have enough money saved," I want you, Cuba and the girls to pack very light; you have to leave this weekend. Ms. Tichele says, "Hold the hell on" I am not leaving you here alone, and then she started her crying shit. "Please Tarsi what is going on," what's wrong baby please talk to me"?

Tarsi just puts his head down and says "mom listen do not ask too many questions it is for your own good.

Tarsi flips on Ms. Tichele "look no more questions mommy!" "You, Cuba, and the girls have to be packed and pack light." Tarsi tells her"; "Shad will come through Sunday with some money" "and the house keys to your new house" Believing and trusting in her son; did as she was asked, packed up the Benz lightly and waited for further instructions. Tarsi had reached out to some folks he had in Seattle, he knew from his earlier days and arranged for a new crib. In addition, even for Cuba to get into rehab once they touched down.

Tarsi is very upset, arranges a meeting with all the top people in his organization. Tarsi explain we have a small problem, not only is this parasite Black trying to muscle in on my operations. However, the maggot threatened my mother. Shad is sitting there thinking, "Damn why the fuck did I drive that Bentley downtown?" Stupid moves get stupid results.

The day has arrived for the sit down, Tarsi connected with a crew uptown, matter of a fact they were his cousins. These niggas were ruthless hustlers but smart. Tarsi could have sent them to pay this nigga Black a visit, which would have started a war. What Tarsi did was value there advise, his cousin "White Sam" was the henchmen a straight killer, his cousin Poncho was the thinker, always advising Tarsi on how to stay low and move right. Tarsi had this one cousin "Black Mike" aka Miz, this was Tarsi's favorite cousin, not only because the nigga got money. However, when Tarsi were a young boy Miz took him under his wing and made him finish school.

They were valued members of his team; he also had "Big Lodge," "he would always tell Tarsi"; "you are better than this street shit, invest your money, stay in school and do something with your life." Then there was "Big "O", "Tajuan", they were more of the observers, always letting Tarsi know what the buzz on the streets. They all showed Tarsi how to move around the snakes. Finally Tarsi can chill his mom is on her way to a new life, his problems in the streets were about to be over.

CHAPTER 16

Tasha is in the car tripping; she is crying saying, "how bad she felt because she had feelings for Tarsi." However, the fucked up thing is Tarsi is feeling Tasha also. So one night Tasha comes over Tarsi and Crystal's crib no one is home but Tarsi. Crystal had taken the kids to a birthday party. Tasha is looking very good she has on that Louis V cat suit with that nice little fat ass with the fat pussy print. Tarsi is looking like "Omg" this bitch is fine as fuck and to top it off she had that long pretty hair, this joint was beautiful for real.

Tasha and Tarsi start kissing next thing Tasha has Tarsi's dick in her mouth he is eating the pussy now it's the fuck on these two freaks are going crazy on each other. Shit is very intense they all on Crystal's bed, on her kitchen floor. I mean Tarsi were straight abusing the pussy. Make things worst Tasha is sleeping over the crib with her sister just so when Crystal falls asleep she can fuck and suck Tarsi's dick. They were doing this shit right while everyone was home asleep.

Then one night the truth came out Tasha goes on to say how she lied she tells him "Tarsi that coke the 100 keys "L" left behind those weren't Mr. Bruno's "L" was too hot in the streets to move them." She goes on to say he figured if he told you that bullshit. You would not fuck the money up. Tarsi is hurt; he is thinking what the fuck "L" lied, Tasha you fucking lied, just to use me but it was too late, Tarsi has the streets on lock. Furthermore, if "L" came home Tasha is now in love with Tarsi this shit is getting all out of control.

Tasha, she caught up for real, she is in love with her own sister's man. This shit is out of control one night Tasha and Tarsi are fucking she says," Tarsi take the rubber off" Tarsi keeps stroking ignoring her. Tasha is in the moment about to reach her climax she screams out "Tarsi I fucking love you and I want your baby too!" Tarsi are thinking; this bitch done lost her mind. However, the pussy was so good; this idiot takes the rubber off. Moreover, bust all inside that warm juicy wet ass gushy.

CHAPTER 17

Sunshine is from Baltimore, shorty, mastered fucking a nigga, then putting her murder game down. The phone rings; Sunshine answers "hey Tarsi baby." Tarsi whispers, "I need to see you ASAP!" We have a special motherfucker who is feeling lonely. The phone hangs up" Sunshine says to herself no problem Daddy I'm on my way"

Later that night, Sunshine touches down, she ask Tarsi "so boss what's the problem"? Tarsi reply, "I need this clown to bust his last nut." Tarsi is very happy now, his 'murder mommy' Sunshine is in town. In addition, remember the fine little messenger bitch Mona? Just happens, while Tarsi driving Sunshine around, explaining their little problem. Who comes walking across the street, Tarsi says; "hey baby that's Black's little messenger right there." Sunshine says, "Damn I wouldn't mind tasting that caramel chocolate." Sunshine, goes on to reassure Tarsi, she says, Boss no problem "I got this please believe me"

Saturday night's, <u>Club Wonder</u> was off the chain; I mean all the hustlers, shot callers; were in the building. Sunshine pulls up in Tarsi's Porsche, everybody was sweating Sunshine, and she was one sexy ass-murdering bitch. Sunshine seizes the opportunity to handle her business; she spots "Mona." Sunshine walks over, offers Mona a drink, not knowing Mona was checking her out also. Sunshine continues to ask Mona," how are you doing"? Mona answers fine thank you, then it dawns on her she never asked her name. Sunshine asked, "So what's you name may I ask"? Shorty, replies Mona, she was (smiling). Sunshine is telling herself; "yeah after I fuck this little bitch and get in her mind," I am going to dead her, this "Ras clad" ass nigga "Black."

Sunshine is all up in Mona's head, finding everything out about this dude Black, now it's time to even the score. "Yeah" so Sunshine got Mona spilling the beans, she "told Sunshine where Black rest his head, keeps his money, and his drugs." The best information of the day was where Black's mom lived at, this even out the score. Then Mona Tells Sunshine she is also fucking this nigga.

She is fucking Black; this is exactly what Sunshine needed to hear.

Sunshine says to Mona 1 night; "let's go out and party," Sunshine's real intentions were for "Black to see how well she looked with that "fat Jamaican ass, knowing most nigga's think with their dicks. Bingo shit works, right away Black is asking Mona "who is your home girl?" "Mona replies this is my girlfriend Sunshine," Black "says nice to meet you Sunshine my name is Black." He then says, "I did not know Mona had such beautiful friends." Sunshine says," nice to meet you also." Therefore, the night goes on, Sunshine is grinding on Mona, doing what she does best; which was throwing that fat ass, oh my God was Sunshine's ass fat!! Black whispers. "Mona, why don't three of us slide up out this spot," Only if he knew he would not be sliding any more fucking fool!

Sunshine and Mona leave the club, with Black's thirsty ass in tow. "Where are we going ladies?" Asked Black, nigga all smiling and shit, Sunshine is straight rocking both of their asses to sleep. Sunshine says, "To fuck nigga that's what you want to do right." This dumb ass nigga Black "replies well of course."

Mona and the crew get back to Black's crib, no time is wasted; Mona and Sunshine start kissing and fingering each other, Black is watching these two bad bitches get there shit off. Sunshine starts eating Mona's pussy and Mona is fucking going crazy, screaming, and moaning. Then Black politely asks, "May I join in"; this nigga whips out his dick, Sunshine starts sucking this nigga's dick; like there is no tomorrow, now all three of them are fucking and sucking, this shit is getting very intense.

In addition, just like that, "Sunshine reaches for her little nickel plated 38 bulldogs with the rubber grip, "she had it tucked in her purse.

"And starts to blast this nigga Black; Pop! Pop!" She blew the white matter out this nigga's head, then she looks at Mona; "like damn you are one fine bitch but I can't have no witness's", she hits her with one shot to the dome. Just like that, Black and Mona were both in the dirt finished. Sunshine hits Tarsi "hey baby, both of them freak ass bitches just bust there last nuts!"

CHAPTER 18

Tasha says, "hey Tarsi in a teasing voice', why haven't you been calling me "you tired of me already nigga." Tarsi answers, "No girl but you know this shit is not right," he goes on to say; "Tasha I love your sister," we are fucking in her house, in her bed as if it's just us involved. Tasha flips out; "Oh it wasn't like that when I'm sucking your dick and you are fucking me!" "Doing whatever, you want too to this pussy." then Tasha says, "Nigga my pussy is not good enough for you anymore"?

Tarsi starts thinking; "This broad is getting real typical on me." "Why are you acting like this, what the fuck is wrong with you?" "Nothing" Tasha answers, "I just love you, Tarsi, and this shit is driving me crazy daddy." Tasha's ass tripping; straight bugging the fuck out, she is on some bullshit literally. This bitch had the nerve to say, "Tarsi I'm the one that put you on, gave you a chance nigga!"

Tarsi responds with; "I will always remember you for that," I thank you. But then he loses his cool and says; "Bitch you are always throwing that shit in my face," He went on to say; "I also fucking stayed looking out for your fucking ass" also," "what more do you fucking want from me?" Tasha answers; "I need my own package", "I am ready to make my own moves." Tarsi get angry, upset, he is really tripping; Tasha is acting like this, he tries to calm her down.

Listen "I have some business to square away, once I return me and you will go on vacation; maybe "Dominican Republic I promise, now Tarsi is all over the place now he has to take care of a lot of bullshit." Tarsi is on the highway, driving thinking; one night trying to get his mind right. He is thinking; "how did I get into this shit"; "This nigga Black wanted to kill him, kidnap his mom; now the streets are talking. Moreover, he is fucking his girl sister." He never expected his life to get crazy like this.

One late night, Tasha calls Tarsi; "Tarsi hey baby I'm sorry for the way I have been behaving", Can you forgive me? Tarsi goes on to say; "I do not know" you might have to make me feel better. Tasha says "I'm on my way baby", by now Crystal is starting to feel some kind of way; I mean her and the kids are good, they have houses, the cars, the clothes, and the money. Nevertheless, Crystal is thinking; Tarsi and Tasha are too fucking close, only if she really knew it would be World War 3.

CHAPTER 19

Sunday arrive, Shad goes over to Ms. Tichele house, knocks on the door; she answers. "Hey," where is Tarsi? "Shad answers"; all he told me was to give you this envelope, address, house key, tell you he loved you. In addition, he will be in touch very soon. Cuba says "baby where are we heading?" Ms. Tichele "yells motherfucker you are lucky you are going anywhere, relax, get the GPS out the glove compartment. "We are heading out west."

In addition, Shad is still on his perpetrating shit, riding around in expensive cars, trunk jewels, expensive gators, and mink coats; after all, he was the reason. Black was gone and Ms. Tichele had to leave town. Tarsi were thinking; laughing, saying to himself, "Shad was a fly nigga, no matter how much perpetrating he did." However, the streets "rules" did not respect him. He never put in any work; one day a nobody, then a superstar the next day, that bred a lot of jealousy and hatred. Nevertheless, Tarsi loved this dude, being as though Tarsi was connected; everyone knew there was off hand policy that followed his man Shad around. However, there was one time, Tarsi almost let his emotions get the best of him, Shad almost caught a bad one.

One of Tarsi's people in the streets hit his jack and said boss, I do not know if this means anything but I just saw Shad and Crystal together and shit did not look kosher. Tarsi said thanks little homie but I'm not worried about that shit right there. A few days passed by, this shit was starting to bother Tarsi, so he asked; "Shad my nigga why were you and Crystal together the other night?" Shad has this oh shit look on his face, he answers Tarsi, "she needed some cash and we couldn't find you." Tarsi is like; "oh okay you know", I was just wondering but in his mind he knows this fag ass motherfucker is lying. Because one thing Tarsi never did was leave Crystal and the kids with no money. Nevertheless, Tarsi model was what goes around comes around. And with all fronting shit this dude was doing in the streets, was just a matter of time, I mean this cat was pushing Bentley's, Benzes all in the fucking hood and Metro task force was dead on his ass.

They had been watching his every move and the truth is they always wanted Tarsi, could never catch him slipping; one night some detectives stop Shad, they are fucking with him saying, "Damn Shad what type of job do you have? One detective says, "Your car game is crazy." Being the arrogant idiot Shad was he tells the cops, "the kind of job you wished you had."

Can you believe this simple asshole just fucked up, jeopardized the whole operation? They were fucking teenagers; barely old enough to drive, making more fucking money, than most grown men their parents age. In addition, dumb ass Shad blows the whole operation out the water with one fucking stupid ass statement. Now the detectives are a little bit uptight and they start fucking with him, saying shit to piss Shad off, they would say "shit like", where is Tarsi anyway, we know he is the boss, you just his fucking bitch. Trying to break Shad, he held his head. Tarsi had some contacts on the force, they gave him a heads up, they are on your man Shad, not letting up, the contact goes on to say "Tarsi get low they are really interested in talking to u also."

Tarsi is thinking; what the fuck should I do, he makes the only choice left as far as he was concerned. He had enough money, figured if they have anything they would have come straight for me. Furthermore, Tarsi is pissed off, all he can "say is this motherfucker Shad" "just blew the whole spot the fuck up." Now, Tarsi just goes and packs some money, looked at his kids one last time and broke out with no goodbye, no explanations just vanished, while on the move, trying to figure out his next plan.

Tarsi met a beautiful young woman, she was nice, and basic she was perfect and right away, their friendship hit it off. Moreover, what Tarsi liked about

her she was going to school and the working type. Tarsi never told her about his past when they first met, they lives clicked right away. After getting to know each other, they moved to Detroit. They attempted to start a new life,

Tarsi had plenty of money but lived a very low-key life.

Life is going great, until one day he gets an unexpected phone call from one of his mom's best friends, Tarsi even called her aunty. The phone rings, Tarsi answers, the voice on the other end. "Hey Tarsi it's Aunt Donna, how are you baby?" Now any other time, he would have been suspect about a call like this. However, as I said Tarsi looked at this woman like a family member, you know the saying "family can be your worst enemy." Aunt Donna goes on to say; "Tarsi I have some peoples I am cool with in Ohio" looking to score some major weight, she goes on to say they want to spend

$80,000 dollars. Tarsi says "damn aunty that sounds nice", but I am not in that life anymore, further more I don't even know anyone with that kind of weight.

Tarsi and his new girl are really enjoying their lives together. Better yet no one know them, they can pay their bills living the American dream. Yeah right the devil never sleeps, Tarsi is sitting up one night; "like damn eighty thousand on one flip." That shit sounds very good, after that flip we would be straight, with the cash I have stashed plus eighty, can open nice little Laundromat, a hair salon and grow old right. Tarsi tell his new girl, "baby my aunt invited us out to Ohio." Tarsi "new girl" answers yes baby, I would love to travel and meet some of your family. Being as though Tarsi was not a show off, he was really exciting to his new Queen.

So the first trip was just a tester, Tarsi took something light a few ounces to test the water and everything went well. In addition, he needed some more time; try to get someone to trust him with so much weight.

Tarsi's new girlfriend did not even realize she was in the middle of some real big boy shit, therefore once they got back to Detroit, and everything is back to regular. The phone rings ring! "Tarsi its auntie baby the voice said," they loved that shit when can you come back? Tarsi is thinking; I 'am being greedy or maybe this one last move, we could grow old right, secured. Just happen, it was a car show in Ohio that weekend and Tarsi's new girl knew how much this nigga loved cars. This was the perfect excuse to go back and he lucked up just happen, some new Columbians were in Detroit and needed some help moving a shipment, so they fronted him the weight he needed to make it happen. Therefore, the train ride to Ohio was going smooth, as planned, they were laughing and joking, had a couple of beers, Tarsi joked about opening up a business one day. However, what happened next would fucking turn both of their lives completely around, come to find out fucking aunty double crossing ass bitch. Had the cops waiting at the train, I mean these bastards were everywhere like a fucking movie, the only thing that saved Tarsi and his shorty. Was when the train was pulling in, Tarsi saw something that looked suspicious he saw a detective talking into a headset, as the train pulled into the terminal. Now it was a matter of life or death, as far as Tarsi was concerned either, get off the train with the work (drugs) and take a chance or leave the drugs on the train and owe the Columbians fifty-five thousand, Tarsi goes with plan 'B' and leaves the coke and good thing he did. Because, when they got off the train, I mean even the ticket agents were undercover agents, that shit was crazy. As soon as Tarsi stepped out weapons were drawn, all you heard was both of you get on the fucking floor now! Yes, you guessed right aunty had done them dirty stinking bitch set Tarsi up to save her own ass.

However, to the agents surprise after searching and questioning Tarsi for hours, after a phone call from Tarsi's high-powered lawyer. They had to release them, In addition, boy was that a good thing. I mean Tarsi's new girl was shaking and crying, she was scared to death. All Tarsi could think; this is a bad fucking dream happened, just because of a lot of greed, could have gotten both of them charged as kingpins.

On the ride home, Tarsi is comforting his girl, tells her some real crazy shit had just taken place. I will explain to you later, Tarsi goes on to say baby, we cannot return to Detroit right now. Tarsi new girl asks why baby. Tarsi; "says we have to go to New York and lay low, that's the safest spot for us right now.

Come to find out these Columbians had heard about Tarsi, his little run in with Ohio finest. They got scared, thought Tarsi was locked up, and even worst he might snitch. Therefore, the Columbians left Detroit, also this was good news for Tarsi, he was able to return, get the money he had stashed, him and his new girl went out to Seattle with Ms. Tichele and Cuba.

Once in Seattle, Tarsi ended up going to college, got his degree in business administration, Ms. Tichele raised the girls, and Cuba went to rehab, cleaned up his act, and became a drug and alcohol counselor. Oh yeah, Tarsi ended up opening one of the largest limousine companies on the West coast.

In addition, turns out Tarsi, his girlfriend settled down, got married, she opened a string of hair salons, Laundromats; they were growing old the right away. In addition, her and Tarsi started their own family, had twins a boy/a girl.

Crystal got over Tarsi and ended up taking their two kids and moving down South.

She never had the physical proof; but she knew Tarsi were creeping with Tasha. Tasha was slinging her package; until her package started slinging her yeah, she made that big mistake of getting high on her own supply, nevertheless she also, got cleaned, and moved out to California and became a make-up artist in Hollywood.

Shad was still on that mission, chasing that childhood fame, took him a minute to understand everything that looks good is not good and not everyone is as fortunate to get out the game without some crucial situations taken place.

As Far as Big "L", there were so many crazy rumors, that he made it out of the game a multi-millionaire, even that he was in witness protection; but the truth is no one ever found out or seen him again, suppose he was seen in

Atlanta Georgia and spotted in Bermuda but none of, it was ever proven fact.

Tarsi was about to catch a flight one night, thinking; how his man Slick use to tell him "It is not what you move it is how you move." Slick was a numbers runner in "A"-Town; he made his millions off the dollar, and a dream game. Even poor folks needed a chance to be a winner. He owned one the most popular jazz spots in "A"-Town we called it Slick Boston's he always looked out and schooled Tarsi to the game.

CHAPTER 20

T arsi is at his limousine company, day dreaming one day, thinking about the lifestyle he lived so fast as a child, a few people came to his mind, he drifts off dreaming how back in the day.

A couple of females come out of the hood doing their numbers, moving bricks, busting their guns. And though most of the female hustlers runs were short, one young girl named Beth Dimples she was getting "bread", if they didn't do it like Beth Dimples they wasn't getting that paper. When she gave a party or cookout shit it was like a big ass fashion show, fly cars, fly nigga's, fly bitches and a lot of balling going on, Beth Dimples was one sexy ass broad, I mean she walked like a fucking stallion, fat ass, she was light skin.

The rumor was her pussy had magical powers; back then, you had a lot of want to be money-getting jokers. However, Beth Dimples this bitch was getting more money than the average person was, she had brains, because back then; one could always tell the ones who would grow up and do some major shit with their lives.

In addition, it was rumored most heavy hitters got there first shipment of bricks on consignment, from Beth Dimples, she hung out with hood superstars like Lloyd Sally and ballers like that.

She was in the major leagues of the cocaine world, she was also smart enough to stack that money and leave town. It was also rumored she moved to the Midwest, started helping the homeless, opened up a soup kitchen. She might have made bad choices as a child, after growing both mentally, spiritually she found herself. Tarsi would often sit alone and reminisce about the life he had lived as a child, would drift off into dream like states.

Like another time, he had a dream about some twins from his old neighborhood, he would think maybe his next venture in life would write movies, so one afternoon while sitting on his front porch he again drifted off; his memory took him on a very interesting journey about these particular "twins."

As Tarsi drift asleep, remembering the twins, these were the perfect definition of men and hustlers, and they were not only young boys getting that bread they were like "Robin Hood" in the hood. What they took from the streets and they also gave back to the streets. One of them were quiet, "kind of sneaky", always a gentleman never stepped on anyone's toes and that shyness got him in good with the ladies, you had the other brother, he was the funny twin, always on his comedian shit saying some crazy shit.

If Tarsi memory served him correctly, by the time they were 17 years old they were millionaires, by the time they graduated high school they were completely out the game.

No one ever knew for real, because if you were not part of their circle, you would never know shit about them anyway. They use to all hustle in this one housing project; it was like a giant open market pharmacy, Tarsi would often slip off, dream about his childhood, wonder what happened to his childhood friends.

Now that Tarsi and his family are out west, things seem to be going as planned. Tarsi started to keep a diary, guessing this was something he felt could help him in his writing, so in his extra time between businesses, he would take different parts of his childhood, and work on creating a movie scripts/book scripts and things were going well.

Therefore, one day he leaves his diary open day and his new wife sits down and reads them, this is what his diary contained.

Tarsi Diary pt. 1

Beth Dimples had left A-Town, moved out to the Midwest she became a caseworker, mentors young girls about the ills, lies the streets falsely paint. Jason Green became an ordained minister, he opened a church named 4th Baptist, he takes in drug addicts, offers homeless somewhere warm to sleep and a hot meal. Jamal Green became a famous restaurant/business owner up and down the east coast.

Tarsi is telling himself he had broken bread, with all types of people, the cash he made funded some important people's lifestyles, and he did favors for many important people.

Tarsi started his diary when he was about to leave, head out west. I have one more thing to get off my chest he wrote in his diary; "I never wanted to doubt my man Shad," even though Tarsi knew Shad had done him dirty. All Tarsi wanted was an apology that was good enough for him.

Tarsi Diary pt. 2

Chip Johnson, now this is a role model for the youth to look up too, Chip came from the same circumstances as many people in the hood. However, what Tarsi admired is that, he kept his eyes on the prize. Chip use to run with Tarsi and his crew but he was smart enough to stay focused, However, he did what all young brothers from the ghetto should do. Chip finished high school went to college.

He even sends kids from the hood to golf camps.

Then you had Ralph Matthews, he also beat the odds he let his basketball skills take him straight out the hood, he also went to college on a full paid scholarship. In addition, that was just the start Ralph also played for the NBA, before his knee injury. Now he's one of the country's leading college basketball coaches, people like this are the real super stars in Tarsi's diary.

Tarsi Diary pt. 3

The game has switched up the streets are finished. The rules are not the same it used to be a code of honor amongst hustlers. Now it was survival of the fittest a doggy dog world. Moreover, any and everybody are calling themselves hustlers. See real hustler didn't want anyone shot, unless deemed necessary. They did not allow the mistreatment of old people, pregnant woman and not saying hustling was the right thing but it was a way of life.

These days you have the young boys with their ass hanging out there pants, back then you even respected the police, yeah you heard me. Because first you knew, the shit you was doing was not right any way. So why would you make enemies with the police or anyone it was business and big business. It's a whole different breed now a dying breed it's shoot um up ask questions later. It's duck season.

Tarsi Diary pt.4

Today you have blood relationships; brothers, sisters, and cousins setting each other up to be murder where is the loyalty in this?

Tarsi Diary pt. 5

See the truth of the matter is you only get one life; yes, you will make some mistakes. Nevertheless, the streets are like a chessboard and most players in the game are just pawns, protecting the real players. That deceitful world of drugs, murder, mayhem, will always mislead you, until you decide, find out the devil is a liar he will give you all your worldly needs for a piece of your soul, the piece that counts the most. One more thing, Tarsi also goes to juvenile detention centers, speaks to the young people about the lies; in hopes of using examples of life, to be an inspiration in helping the youth, deter them from making the same mistakes so many people have made. It is no such word as loyalty, in the streets either you go to jail, your man is fucking your wife, you leave some cash, your man, or your chick spending it. The truth of the matter; the ones who succeed are the ones who go to school and get an education. Moreover, let us say you have enough paper from getting your hustle on get out the streets before it is too late. Do the math how many jokers do you know in the streets get out successfully. "It's a no win situation" See the truth is most people born in the ghettos are misled and most of the time it is by our own peers jokers who have already fucked their own lives up.

Ask yourself how do you love your brother or sister if you are willing to sell them poison, then ask yourself why does a young brother or sister think it's acceptable to kill another human being over a block they don't even own. We have to keep it real with ourselves first. Before we attempt to show anyone else with foolish actions how real, we are pretending to be. Forget looking for loyalty from the streets, show loyalty to yourself, your family look up to the jokers contributing positive elements to your community.

Tarsi Diary pt.6

This is to all my brothers. Please know that we are more than a statistic, killing each other with guns, selling drugs that doesn't make you a man, it just helps you contribute to ignorant behavior and destruction of our own communities.

Tarsi Diary pt.7

To all my sisters, no matter your color or creed. You are all queens and you deserve to, be treated as one, you are neither a bitch nor a slut and you deserve to be respected as a queen However, it first starts with self-respect.

Therefore, Tarsi's new bride is really shocked, and impressed after reading her husband's diary, and at dinner encourages him to pursue a hobby in writing. In addition, Tarsi is thinking maybe this is something that would help him past the time and occasionally revisit his yester years.

The truth starts with self!!

The truth will set you free in mind, body, and soul.

The statistics for a male in the ghetto
That you will be either dead or in prison by the age of 25
We can beat those numbers.

In order to make a difference.
We first have to be willing to change ourselves.

To once, be lost to the ill ways, lies, the streets falsely display, find your positive energy, inner peace. This makes you a Found Son, Found Daughter.

PEACE LIVES IN SPIRT NOT IN FLESH.

~About the Author~

Thomas C was born in Bronx New York, from there he moved around, to several places as a child including; Los Angles California (Inglewood), then relocated to Atlanta Georgia, before moving to Atlantic City, NJ with his mother and step-father. As a child he grew up on the rough, mean streets of New Jersey, visiting summers back in New York City where he learned many tricks of many trades, some he was not so proud of. He knew one day this life he had to escape.

Thomas C writes under his last initial "C", only for the purpose of, reminding himself of both lives he was once lived. When he was young and living a dark life-style. It was under the assumed last name of his step father. But once he became of age, learned the last name of his real dad, which also started with the letter C. He took on this last name, with it. He adapted a new, positive way of living, thinking.

After suffering, surviving some major health issues. He was hospitalized and this is where he decided to become a writer. So he could offer help and hope in maybe deterring especially the youth from traveling the road he once traveled. Furthermore, too let others know it's never too late to turn your life around. In 2009 Thomas C early retired from State of New Jersey Juvenile Justice Commission, set out on his own mission to help others. Also in 2012 he became an ordained non-domination minister. He holds several certificates from the State of New Jersey. He also is an avid soul food cook.

Also to his credits he has written a children's book titled. 'Just Because My Shell Is Different', an inspirational poetry book titled 'Poetry of my Mind'.

He has a saying that he often uses. "He once ran with devil." "But now he walks with God."

Thomas C is a fictional, inspirational story teller with some stories to tell. He is a husband, father, grandfather, brother, friend, son, grandson and most of all. He is just plain Thomas C the Book Author. Also he paints symbolic artwork, drawings which can be seen on Fine Art of America.

Also by Thomas C.

Also by Thomas C.

Please post your reviews on amazon.com. Thanks for your support and feedback in advance.
Sincerely,
Thomas C.